HAPPY
HALLOWEEN

HAPPY HALLOWEEN

Edgar J. Hyde

CCP

© 1998 Children's Choice Publications Ltd

Text supplied by Simon Bedding

ISBN 1-902012-16-X

Printed and bound in the UK

Contents

Chapter 1

It was Wednesday morning and Samantha, James and Mandy were preparing for Saturday. Saturday was the thirty-first of October – Halloween. The three children were going away to a small village for a few days and were leaving tomorrow, but this wasn't going to stop them trick-or-treating, which was why they were making their costumes now, instead of at the last minute like other years. Their school was closed for urgent repairs over the coming weeks so they were making the most of this welcome holiday.

Samantha (known as Sam), the eldest, was thirteen with an unruly mop of blond hair. Mandy and James were twelve and twins. They looked very different from each other (though, as Mandy had shoulder length blonde hair and James' hair was light brown and short.

"I really don't know what costume to wear – I don't want to look stupid," sighed James.

"That's okay," replied Sam, "you look stupid anyway."

"You're so funny you make me want to laugh out loud," retorted James sarcastically.

"Why, thank you James," said Sam, pretending not to have heard the sarcasm in her brother's voice, "and just looking at you makes me quite hysterical."

"Oh, shut-up you two," said Mandy, "we're getting too old to do this, so it's going to be the last year we get free treats."

"Well I only go along to look after you two," said Sam.

"You do not," cried James indignantly, "you come with us because you like free sweets and stuff as much as me and Mandy."

"Well, when I don't go you never give me any," said Sam defensively.

"Anyway," said Mandy quickly, before the two started arguing again, "what are you two going to wear?"

"Like I said, I don't know," James answered.

"I'm just going to pop a couple of vampire teeth in and wear black," said Sam. "I'd never live it down going trick-or-treating with a sheet with holes in it over my head."

"I was thinking something like that which is why

I'm going to overdo the dark eye shadow," said Mandy.

"I'm going as Dracula – I'm going to put some green face paint on, wear a cape, put some fangs in my mouth and I'm going to gel my hair in a Dracula style," said James.

Sam and Mandy looked at him in disbelief. Finally Sam said:

"Are you sure you want to go trick-or-treating by yourself?"

"No, I'm going with you," replied James.

"Not like that you're not," said Mandy firmly. "For goodness sake, you said you didn't want to look stupid."

"Okay then, what shall I wear?" asked James.

"The same as me," Sam answered.

James shrugged and said:

"Okay, if it makes you happy, oh boring one."

Just as James made a disgusting face that involved shoving his fingers up his nose and sticking out his tongue, the children's mother came into the room.

"I'm always telling people that you're the handsome one in the family James," she said.

James blushed and took his fingers out of his nostrils.

"Have you three had breakfast yet?"

"Not yet Mum," replied Mandy.

"I wondered why I was so hungry," said Sam, "let's cook a fry-up."

"Alright," said James, "I'm starving."

"Fine, but don't make a mess," said Mum

Downstairs in the kitchen the three children quickly set about with the frying pans and soon the wonderful smell of bacon filled the air. Shortly, Sam, James and Mandy were settling down to sausages, eggs, bacon, mushrooms, and fried tomatoes. They ravenously tucked in, and soon they were sitting back in their chairs, their stomachs filled.

"That was lovely," Sam said in a satisfied voice, "there's nothing like a good fried breakfast to really fill you up."

"And that was nothing like a good fried breakfast," replied James.

"You think you're so funny don't you?" Sam said to her brother, "But really, you're very, very boring."

"In your opinion," James answered.

"What shall we do today then?" asked Mandy, changing the subject.

"Well, first I'm going to pack my clothes for the weekend," Sam said.

"Okay then, let's all do it now and be thinking of

what to do with the rest of the day," Mandy replied.

It took the three of them only an hour to pack their clothes. At eleven-thirty they were in the lounge watching the television. Suddenly Sam leapt up and said:

"*That's* what I forgot."

"What did you forget?" asked Mandy.

"My vampire teeth, I forgot to pack them – I'd better do it now or I'll forget again."

Five minutes later he was back downstairs again, holding something at arm's length.

"What's that?" asked James.

"It's my teeth, I think they've gone a bit mouldy," replied Sam.

"Yuck," Mandy said, "how did that happen?"

"I tried to eat lasagne with them in last year and forgot to clean them," answered Sam.

"Are you going to wear them?" asked James.

"Of course not," Sam said, "but here, you can have them."

Sam threw the mouldy teeth into James' lap.

"Ugh!" James cried, throwing them at Mandy.

"James!" Mandy shouted, throwing the teeth out of the window.

"Are you going to come with me to get some

more?" asked Sam.

"Not now!" said James, "you must be joking. *Supersonic Power Ninjas* is about to start!"

"Come on," coaxed Sam, "you can get some new teeth as well."

"Okay then, let me grab some money and we'll go."

"I might as well come too," said Mandy, following her brothers out of the room, "I've got nothing better to do."

James rather liked the local joke shop. He pretended that he was much too mature for dressing up and for whoopee cushions, foaming sugar, stink bombs, invisible ink and all the rest – but while the other two were distracted by some creepy masks and a squabble over who had the longest Dracula fangs, he sneakily bought himself some silly tricks, and some fake-blood capsules so that he could be the best vampire.

Afterwards, the three children spent the day lounging around the house. They didn't get to bed too late, so that they could be up early the next morning.

Chapter 2

The next morning the family were up at about seven o'clock, and were getting the last things ready for the long drive. They had breakfast at nine o'clock and set off half an hour later. The journey was long, and for the most part, boring. The three children tried to play a game of travel Monopoly in the back of the car, but the pieces kept on falling off of the board, so in the end they gave up and talked among themselves.

"I can't wait to get there," said Sam, "I wonder what the village is like?"

"It's quite old I think," said Mandy, "you know, one of these places where they have only one phone in the whole village."

"It sounds really exciting," said James, sarcastically, "I hope they've heard of Halloween there."

"I hope they don't mind us trick-or-treating around there either," said Sam.

"It's not *that* backward there," said Mum, turning round, "I'm sure they have more than one phone in the village."

"Well I hope so," Sam replied.

As it turned out, the village, although old, had actually moved with the times. The cottage they were renting was situated on the outskirts and had electricity, running water and a telephone. The village was quite large, and was used by commuters going into the city each day. In fact, the village even had its own little station.

"What were you saying about the village being backward?" James asked Mandy, jokingly.

"Okay, so I was wrong," Mandy replied.

"Is this the cottage then?" asked Sam, as they pulled up outside a ramshackle, thatched house, which was situated alongside a rutted and pitted road.

"Yep, we're here," answered Dad.

The cottage looked very old with lichen-covered walls made from different sized and shaped stones. The windows were leaded. Although the cottage looked very picturesque, Sam couldn't help sensing something sinister. She couldn't explain why she felt this, as the cottage looked anything but sinister. Suddenly, out of the corner of her eye, Sam saw a movement behind one of the dark windows. She looked straight at the window but nothing else happened.

Sam shivered. She was just being silly, she told herself – no-one else had noticed anything – it was probably just a reflection of one of the family.

"Come on Sam, get your bag out of the boot," said Dad, "we're going in, unless you really want to stay out here all night."

Sam shook herself and hauled her bag out of the boot of his Dad's car. After thinking for a moment, she said to her Dad:

"Dad, is anyone else staying in the cottage?"

"There's hardly enough room for the five of us, let alone anybody else," replied Dad.

"Not even a housekeeper or anyone?"

"Not that I'm aware. Why?"

"Oh, no reason," replied Sam.

Inside, the cottage had the musty smell of antique furnishings. In some of the rooms there were panelled walls that looked very old. It was strange that a cottage of this size should have things like panelled walls which didn't seem to fit in at all. Sam commented on this to her Dad.

"Apparently, years ago a man lived here who was fairly rich," said Dad. "He was also pretty eccentric and did the place up like a stately home inside."

"But what was he doing living in a cottage if he was rich?" asked Sam.

"Well, like I said, he was an eccentric," replied Dad. "You know how these rumours go, people said he dabbled in the occult and all sorts of stuff."

"What happened to him then?" asked Sam.

"Well, I was talking to the lady in the post office and she said he accidentally 'magicked' himself away," answered Dad. "Of course, you can't believe everything you hear can you?"

Mum, who had been in the kitchen with Mandy and James, came out into the corridor and said to Sam and Dad:

"James is making a nice cup of tea you two, do you want a cup?"

"I'm dying for a cup," replied Dad.

"Count me in," chipped in Sam.

They followed her into the kitchen, which had a low, beamed ceiling. Mandy was sitting at the kitchen table and James was pouring the hot water into the teapot.

"Two more for tea James," said Mum.

"Righto," said James, "I'll just give it a stir and leave it for a couple of minutes before I pour it out."

"Don't make mine too strong."

Chapter 2

"Aw – would diddums like Jamesy Wamesy to blow on it for her too?"

Sam didn't rise to the bait. She was too preoccupied with the story about the old eccentric man.

"No thank you dearest brother – just two sugars and some milk."

She sat down on the bench at the kitchen table, which was uneven, wooden and clearly very old.

"Isn't the cottage lovely?" said Mum enthusiastically.

"It is isn't it," agreed Mandy.

"It was lucky we got it at this short notice," said Dad.

"I'm looking forward to tomorrow night," James said.

"So am I," said Sam.

"What time do you think we ought to go out?" asked Mandy.

"I reckon about eight-ish," replied Sam, "in that way we can get a good two hours in."

"I agree," said James, "we ought to get a good hoard by that time."

"So what should the trick part of the trick-or-treat be?" asked Mandy.

"I hadn't given that much thought," Sam admitted. "I supposed we could put rice through people's letter boxes."

"As tricks go, I have to say that putting rice through the letter box is pretty tame," said James, "how about egging their houses?"

"James, that's horrible," said Mandy. "What about water balloons," she added with a wicked laugh.

"I think that we should stick to rice," said Sam.

"What about rice pudding then?" said Mandy.

"How's that tea coming along James?" asked Dad.

"Okay, okay, I'm doing it," replied James.

After their brief cup of tea, the family chose their rooms. The girls shared a room while James had his own. The rooms were all on the ground floor as the cottage didn't have an upstairs, only an attic, which the three children were intent upon exploring the next day.

After unpacking their clothes and settling in, Sam, James and Mandy sat in the small lounge, reading magazines. After only a few minutes, Mum came in and said:

"Could one of you nip out before the shops close and get a loaf of bread – I saw a grocer's on the way here – it won't take you five minutes."

"Okay Mum," said Sam.

"Thanks Sam," Mum replied, before giving her some money and leaving the room.

Chapter 2

"Come on you two," said Sam, "let's go"

"I'm sure Mum said 'could *one* of you go'" said James.

"So you're not certain then," said Sam. "Come on."

"Okay, coming," said James, shrugging.

"Mandy, come on."

"Oh, sorry," she said, pretending she hadn't heard, "I didn't hear you."

"Yeah right," Sam replied.

The walk took only ten minutes. The shop was quite modern and seemed to sell everything you could ever want. Sam picked up a loaf of bread and went to the counter to pay for it.

"That'll be forty pence, please," the checkout woman said to Sam. "I ain't seen you before – are you new 'ere?"

"We're staying in a cottage down the road for a few days," said Mandy.

"Oh. Which one?" asked the woman as Sam paid her the money. "Not the old wizard's cottage."

"Wizard's cottage?" asked James.

"That's just what we call it around 'ere 'cos of the guy who used to live there was meant to practise black magic and one day . . . he just disappeared."

"We heard about that," said Mandy.

"I don't believe it of course," said the woman not too convincingly. "So you *are* staying there then?"

"Yes – until Monday," answered Sam.

"Well, like I said, I don't usually believe silly old stories like that," the woman told him, "but I wouldn't like to stay there over Halloween all the same – not with the things that they say used to go on there," she added with a worrying look in her eye.

"It's only a story," said James, "Halloween or not."

"Well," replied the checkout woman, slightly annoyed, "there are stories about strange things happening at the cottage – especially around this time of year."

"What strange things?" asked Mandy, her eyes wide with fright.

"Oh I don't like to worry you. Still, rather you than me."

"Thanks for the bread," said Sam, finishing the conversation. "We'd better go now – bye."

"Goodbye, then," replied the woman turning away from the desk. Did Sam notice a look of amusement in the woman's face?

Outside, the three began talking.

"You didn't have to be rude James," said Sam.

"She was just trying to scare us," her brother replied, "we're not kids!"

"Well, she's certainly freaked me out a bit," said Mandy, shivering. "I wonder what the strange things were that she was talking about."

"It was the way she pretended she didn't believe it that got me," said Sam.

"You two are pathetic, she didn't scare me at all," snorted James.

Soon the three were back at the cottage. They spent the rest of the evening settling in, playing board games and watching television before going to bed at eleven-thirty. With the lights out in their room, the girls spoke.

"I'm looking forward to Saturday night," said Mandy.

"Too right – I could do with all those treats," replied Sam.

"Are you going to pig out on the sweets and stuff all at once?" asked Mandy.

"Well, I'll probably try to ration it for about half an hour – then I'll give in and pig out on the lot," answered Sam.

The girls lay in their beds for a while before Sam said to Mandy:

"Wouldn't it be cool if you could meet a real ghost or something Mandy."

"If you say so," replied Mandy. "Although, to be honest, I'd probably wet myself."

The girls lay in the dark for a further few seconds, listening to the wind whistling slightly through the eaves and the soft splatter of rain against the window panes. Outside, the sky was an inky black, with few stars showing.

"Goodnight Mandy," said Sam.

"Night Sam," said Mandy, yawning.

Within a few minutes, all that could be heard in the bedroom, apart from the wind and the rain from outside, was the soft snoring of the two sisters.

Chapter 3

The next morning, the light shining through the window in the girls' bedroom was cold, harsh and soulless. The light fell upon the slumbering figures of Sam and Mandy. Suddenly, Sam's alarm clock sounded. The regular and insistent electronic beeping eventually woke up Mandy, who threw one of her pillows across the room at Sam to wake her up. Sam grunted a little, before turning over and muttering something to herself in her sleep. She continued snoring.

Mandy was forced to climb out of bed and go over to Sam's bedside table and turn the alarm off herself. She winced as the cold air struck her warm body. After switching off the alarm, Mandy picked her pillow up from off of the floor and swung it at Sam's head, awakening her with a start.

"Good morning – this is your 9 a.m. alarm call," said Mandy with the voice of a Dalek, as she whacked Sam with the pillow again.

"I didn't hear the alarm," exclaimed Sam.

"I noticed," Mandy said, jumping back into bed and snuggling up into her duvet, trying to regain some of her warmth. "Don't fall asleep again."

"I won't," replied Sam, yawning.

They both went back to sleep.

An hour later, at ten o'clock, James came in.

"Wake up!" he shouted, grinning to himself as both of his sisters rubbed their eyes grumpily and squinted at him.

"Go away you horrible boy," groaned Sam.

"Not if I can help it," said James. James had bought himself a present in the joke shop while the girls looked at Halloween masks. It was a water pistol – and he squirted them both in their faces.

"James, I hate you," said Sam, "next time you're asleep I'm going to remember this."

"Yeah," added Mandy, "and I'm going to go into your room and pour a bucket of water over you."

"What a pleasant 'Good Morning' from my loving sisters," said James sarcastically. "Come on lazy pigs – get up or *I* will come in and pour a bucket of water over you."

"You are truly evil," said Sam and threw her pillow at him.

"I love to see my sisters suffer," he laughed.

Chapter 3

"Well you've certainly achieved that," said Sam, now fully awake. "If you want to be forgiven, you could make me a cup of tea."

"And for me," Mandy chipped in from under her duvet.

"Okay pig-girls – don't go to sleep again though," he said.

By the time James returned with the two piping cups of tea, his sisters were up and getting ready for the day. Sam grabbed a cup from his hands and ran as fast as she could without spilling it into the bathroom, shouting:

"Me first into the shower!"

"Damn!" exclaimed Mandy, "I was about to do that."

"By the time you've finished your tea she'll be out," replied James.

"What I want to know is, how she can drink a cup of tea in the shower," said Mandy

"Put it like this," said James.

"What?" asked Mandy.

"She drinks about five times as much tea as she would if she drank it in the bath."

"Does she?" she said, completely missing the joke. "How?"

James looked at her to see if she was pretending to not get it. She wasn't.

"Mandy, it was a . . ." began James and thought better of explaining the joke.

"What was a what?" Mandy asked. "What was it and what were you trying to tell me what what was."

James ran the sentence through his head to try to make sense of it the second time around. Nope, it still didn't make any sense at all.

"Mandy," he said.

"Yes?" she replied.

"Shut up."

Sam came out of the shower and Mandy finally had a chance to get washed. Eventually the three were in the kitchen with Mum and Dad, eating breakfast.

"We're thinking of going to the garden centre which we passed on the way here today," said Dad.

"Sounds . . . fun," replied Sam searching for an appropriate description.

"Are you three going to tag along?"

"Sorry Dad," said James, "I'd love to but I've got to . . ."

He faltered, but thankfully Sam came to the rescue.

". . . to do some school project work and I'm helping him as I did the same project last year."

Chapter 3

"Are you coming Mandy?" asked Dad.

"No, I'm doing the same project as James since we're in the same year and I think that Sam would be able to help me an awful lot," was her rapid reply.

"Isn't it amazing that suddenly everyone has project work which needs to be done, just when we're about to go to the garden centre," said Dad jokingly.

"I suppose they must have been planning it for ages," Mum replied, pretending to be talking to Dad as if Sam, James and Mandy weren't there.

"Before you do your 'project', you three can clear up the breakfast things," Dad said.

The children groaned.

"Bye, bye," said Dad.

"Bye," said the three children, as their parents left the room.

"Isn't it amazing how parents find garden centres so fascinating," said James, "I find them boring, boring, boring."

"I know what you mean," agreed Sam, "I mean, they actually go around them with smiles on their faces as they see – I don't know – this season's most fashionable begonia, or—or—or the lesser-spotted-Outer-Mongolian Rhododendron in electric blue, with speed lines and a soft top."

"Whatever," said Mandy, giving her sister an odd look. "Anyway, let's get the clearing away finished and then we can get a good look around the house."

Soon the children were finished and were planning what to do for the day.

"I know," began Sam, "Let's have a look at the attic, I'm sure there must be something up there."

"Okay," said Mandy, "Let's use a stool to get up there – the ceiling isn't too high."

Sam grabbed a stool and her brother and sister followed her into the hallway where there was a loft hole in the ceiling.

Sam settled the stool beneath the hole and stood upon it. She reached up, pushed the square of wood aside and pulled herself into the attic.

"Mandy, can you fetch the candles and matches from the larder in the kitchen? It's pitch black up here."

James was next, followed by Mandy with the candles.

They lit three candles. The attic was quite small. It was also quite empty, with only a couple of boxes close to the hole. Sam went over to the boxes, followed by James and Mandy. She opened one box, but all that was inside was the usual attic junk – non-matching china, assorted hideous ornaments

Chapter 3

and other similar things. The other box had the same sort contents as the first.

"Nothing," said Sam disappointed, "well, nothing interesting at any rate."

"I read somewhere that all sorts of thing were hidden in the thatch in the olden days," said James. "This thatch looks fairly old, how about a look around?"

"As there is nothing else of much interest to do, I agree," replied Sam.

The three children spent about fifteen minutes looking all over the attic with no success. Eventually James said:

"Nothing – I say that we give up and do something else. Obviously the people who lived here didn't want to hide stuff in the attic."

"I agree," said Mandy.

"Okay," agreed Sam reluctantly, "Let's just look in this corner and then we can go down again."

As she crossed the attic she said:

"It's a shame really, I thought we might find something old do with the old occultist."

"What? Like a spell book?" said James.

Sam caught a movement out of the corner of her eye, near to where she was searching, as James said this.

"Yeah," said Sam, as she reached the area where

she had seen the movement. She rummaged around a bit until suddenly, she felt a solid, square object beneath her groping hand.

"I've found something!" she cried.

"Yeah right," replied James.

"No honestly," said Sam, pulling from out of the crevice where she was searching, a battered, leather bound book.

"What is it?" asked Mandy, coming over to where Sam was.

"No, wait, there's more," Sam said, pulling out a small, leather, old fashioned money bag. It was bulging.

She opened it – inside there were three large, coloured, translucent, cut stones.

Sam looked at the book. There was no title on the cover but inside, the first dog-eared page proclaimed the book to be:

Thee Mysticke Artes Of Magicke
&
Manye Popular & Interestinge Spelles

"That spell book James," said Sam, "were you thinking of something like this?"

"I can't believe it – a real spell book!" said James for the hundredth time.

"I wonder if they work?" asked Sam.

"Hang on you two – I don't like this – this could be dabbling in the occult," said Mandy.

"Don't be silly Mandy, they don't *really* work, you don't *really* think that there's such a thing as magic," scoffed James. "Go on, say one Sam."

"Don't!" said Mandy.

"Go on," coaxed James.

"I'll just try a little one then," said Sam, trying to please both of them at once.

"I really wouldn't if I were you – but it's up to you," said Mandy," idly playing with one of the stones from the bag.

"Okay then, let's see . . ." Sam began, "right – here's one, an illusion…"

"Woo-woo-woo-woo…" said James, imitating the music out of the *Twilight Zone*.

"Addi, cysti, adonis, crytis, chi," uttered Sam. Nothing happened.

"See Mandy, nothing to worry about," laughed James.

"Hang on," said Sam, "it's a little difficult to read – ah, I see, I need to use the Rune stone and draw a pentagon in the air with it and name the object I want to create the image of when I have done that,"

"Come on Sam," said James, "you're acting like you believe in this stuff."

"Shhh!" said Sam, "now, which one is the Rune stone? How about his green one?"

He picked it up and uttered the words again, whilst drawing the shape of a pentagon in the air with the green stone. The stone left a green trail, until it had taken the shape of a pentagon. Sam then said:

"Vase!"

Sam pictured the vase in her head.

Suddenly an arrow appeared out of nowhere with a green flash, hovered for a second, and then flew straight towards Sam's head. She put the spell book up to her face for protection. The arrow struck it and disappeared with another green flash. Sam looked down at the book. There wasn't a mark on it.

"They don't really work, you don't really think that there's such a thing as magic!" growled Sam, mimicking her brother. "Then what the heck was that?!"

"That was amazing Sam," cried James, "I didn't think you had it in you!"

"She nearly got killed James," said Mandy, "Anyway I thought you said 'vase' Sam, not 'arrow'."

Mandy shook her head in disbelief before eventually saying:

"Wow! You did magic!"

Sam opened the book at the beginning and read the first page.

Chapter 3

" 'To the practitioner of the art of magic, a word of warning. Magic is an art where absolute concentration is required – mistakes can prove deadly to the unwary scholar. There are many things you should not attempt, which are outlined in this tome, but the one thing which you must never do, is use the incorrect magic stones in the spells. If the incorrect stone is used in a spell, the resulting consequence can be disastrous and, if you are lucky, you will die quickly. Even the most minor spell can have dangerous consequences if used with the incorrect stone. You have been warned – magic is a dangerous art and should be approached with every caution.' "

"I think," said Mandy slowly, "That we were very lucky then."

"I think you're right," said Sam. "I wonder which stones are whi— oh, there's an explanation here, telling us what is what. The green stone is the Talis stone, the red stone is the Rune stone and the blue one is the Pikez stone. I think that we should approach this with care and read the book before we try anything else."

"You're going to try *more*?" cried Mandy. "I would have thought that nearly being killed would have warned you off magic for good!"

"Don't be stupid Mandy," said James, "Sam

knows what she's doing – and besides, I want to have go as well."

Mandy couldn't think of what to say. Eventually she just said:

"You're nuts, you're both nuts, but I'll go along with it for now. Besides, I can't deny that this is all very intriguing – do you think I could have a go?"

Sam grinned and said:

"I knew that was the real reason Mand."

"Okay, so where shall we go from here?" Mandy asked.

"Let's all read it now," suggested James.

"Okay then, we'll do it in the kitchen at the table – in that way we'll all be able to read it," said Sam.

The three children spent the next hour reading the beginning of the spell book and discussing it. One thing interested them greatly.

"It says that to do magic you have to have a natural talent at it in the first place," said Sam.

"I was reading that," said James. "And you do know what that means . . .?"

"What?" asked Mandy. "That Sam is naturally gifted at magic?"

"I guess so," Sam said, grinning broadly. "Why don't we try that spell again?"

"Okay then Sam, but this time I want a go," said James.

"If you have the talent that is," said Sam.

"Addi, cysti, adonis, crytis, chi," said James, drawing the shape of a pentagon in the air with the red stone this time. A red pentagon temporarily flared in the air as James said:

"Ball."

He pictured the ball in his head but nothing happened.

"Here let me," said Sam, taking the stone. She went through the ritual again, finishing with the word:

"Ball."

Sam too pictured the ball in the air and this time a bright yellow ball appeared in front of her where the pentagon had been. She reached out to touch the image, but her hand passed straight through it, and it quickly dissolved into nothing.

"Looks like I've got the talent then," said Sam smugly, "bad luck James."

"Here let me try," said Mandy, snatching the stone from Sam. She too went through the motions, but ended up with the same result as James.

"Oh well Mandy," said Sam, "good try but you didn't quite do it."

"Oh shut up Sam," said Mandy. "You're just lucky, that's all."

"Luck?" said Sam, "It's not luck, just pure skill!"

"Yeah, whatever," muttered James bitterly.

"Seriously though," said Mandy, "what are you going to do now?"

"I don't know, practise it a bit I guess," replied Sam.

"Are you sure?" asked Mandy, "remember what happened to that other guy . . ."

"I'll be careful, okay," answered Sam.

"Okay, as long as you remember," Mandy told her. "Now, I don't know about you two but I'm starving."

Sam looked at her watch. It was half past one and she suddenly realised she was hungry. As Mandy was going over to the cupboard to see if there was anything to eat, Sam stopped her and said:

"I'll make us some lunch shall I?"

"Are you sure?" asked Mandy, suddenly filled with doubt.

"I've got to try sometime," replied Sam.

She opened the book and scanned the contents. The contents listed many spells and it took her a while to find one which sounded appropriate.

"Creating Objects Through Raw Magic," she read, "Page one hundred and seventeen."

Sam turned to the correct page and read through the spell. She whistled though her teeth and said:

Chapter 3

"All that just to get lunch?"

"Let me see that," said James, tugging the book from his sister's hands.

"It's like a recipe," he said.

"I don't even know what half of this stuff is," said Sam, "I won't be able to do half the stuff I wanted to."

"Pass the book," said Mandy, sitting down opposite them.

As James passed it to her, the book suddenly tumbled from his hands onto the kitchen table. As it landed, a scrap of paper, brown with age, fluttered from between the pages and wafted to the floor. Sam got to it first.

"What is it?" asked James.

"It's a set of instructions I think," replied Sam.

"What does it say?" asked Mandy.

"Look, let's sit down and I'll read it out, okay?"

"Okay," replied Mandy.

The three sat down and Sam began reading:

" 'To My Successor,' " she began, " 'By now you will have found the spell book and bag of magic stones. The 'ingredients' to all the spells contained within the book are hidden, protected threefold from the wrong people. If you are truly dedicated to practising the art of Magic, and you have the ability, you will discover the ingredients hidden in a place where you, and you alone, can find them, but only when you are ready to use them. Practise the lesser spells first, you know when you will be ready to progress to harder and more dangerous spells.

Finally, you will have heard that I killed myself through magic – I didn't – I just went somewhere else.

Good luck and be cautious as you walk the path of magic.

Yours, Winston Bellingford.' "

Sam stopped reading.

"Wow," said James, "looks like he was expecting you Sam."

"Oh well, looks like lunch is whatever we find in the cupboards then," sighed Sam.

"I'm glad," said Mandy, "knowing you Sam, you would have probably created a cyanide meringue."

"Thank you for your words of confidence Mandy."

"That's okay," she replied, grinning.

After lunch, Sam, James and Mandy went into the lounge to study the book of spells some more.

"Try moving something with magic," suggested James.

"Okay. What?" asked Sam.

"How about that cushion on the sofa," said Mandy.

Chapter 3

"I'll try, if I can find the right spell," said Sam.

She looked through the contents in the spell book until she found the word 'levitation'. She flicked to the appropriate page and read the spell. Fortunately it didn't require anything more than a few words and a magic stone. Sam read the spell again before standing up to prepare herself to say it.

"Stand back," she said, "here goes."

She picked up the appropriate stone – the blue 'Pikez' stone, and drew a blue pentagon in the air as she uttered the words:

"Chelon, levita, greyshun, avatar."

Pointing her finger at the cushion, she slowly raised her arm. The cushion lifted into the air. Sam moved her arm left and the cushion followed it. Sam moved her arm up and the cushion floated higher. Willing the cushion towards her, Sam made the cushion move closer, until it was hovering in front of her finger.

"Okay, how do I stop it?" she asked James.

James picked up the book and said:

"It doesn't say."

"It must do somewhere," replied Sam.

"I can't find it."

"Try not pointing at the cushion," suggested Mandy.

Sam did so and the cushion remained where it

was.

"How did we stop the illusion?" asked James.

"It evaporated when Sam touched it," said Mandy.

Sam touched the cushion. The cushion squashed where her finger touched it, but didn't drop out if the air.

"Try pulling it Sam," said James.

Sam tried to pull the cushion from the air but it remained immobile. The cushion squashed more and more as Sam pulled harder and harder, but remained in the same place. Sam let go and the cushion regained its shape.

Just then, the sound of the front door being opened by their Dad caused the children to look at each other in alarm.

"What shall we do?" asked Sam, wide eyed.

"Quick, levitate it onto the sofa," said Mandy.

Sam pointed at the cushion and moved her hand down to point at the sofa. The cushion remained in the same place. Sam moved her hand back up to re-point her finger at the cushion but as she did so the sofa lifted a foot from the ground.

"What are you doing?" cried James, as he heard the sound of Mum and Dad talking in the hallway outside the lounge.

Sam quickly moved her arm down, lowering the

sofa to the ground. She clenched her hand and moved it away from the sofa. Fortunately the sofa didn't move, but it also didn't move when James tried to push it.

"Great, well done Sam," muttered Mandy, as she tugged ineffectually at the cushion.

At that moment Dad walked in, followed by Mum.

"We've just come in to get my wallet," he said, "I forgot to take it out with me, so the garden centre are holding the plants we are buying until I get it."

Dad looked at Mandy, pretending to hold the cushion.

"What *are* you doing Mandy?" he asked.

"Er – I . . . er . . . James said that girls were weaker than boys and I said they weren't and he said prove it and I said okay, I bet I can hold this cushion out in front of me for longer than you."

"If you say so," said Dad slightly unconvinced, "anyway, we're off out again, okay?"

"Fine Dad," said Sam, "Bye."

"And have some lunch," said Mum as she and Dad left the room.

"We've had it Mum," called James.

"Alright – bye!" replied Mum, closing the front door behind her.

After a few seconds they heard the car starting up and driving off. A few more seconds passed before Mandy said:

"Well, that was close."

"So cushions are so heavy that girls have trouble holding them, am I right?" asked James.

"Well it was better than what you said," replied Mandy.

"I didn't say anything," said James.

"That's what I mean," said Mandy.

"What I want to know," said Sam, changing the subject, "is how to get the cushion down."

"Read the book," said Mandy.

"James said there was nothing in there," Sam answered.

"Read the introduction to this section of the book," said Mandy. "Look, in the contents. Levitation is under the title of Interacting with Objects."

"Okay," Sam replied.

Sam spent the next few minutes reading the introduction to the section, until she came across a paragraph concerning the ending of spells.

"It says here that some of the spells in the section require an additional word to complete the spell," she said.

"What word's that?" asked Mandy.

"It's quite difficult to say. Genimi? Denimi?

Djenimi?" Upon the last word, the cushion fell from the air and the sofa, which James had being leaning against, rolled away from him on its castors. He landed upon the floor with a thud.

"Ouch," he exclaimed, "thanks a lot Sam,"

"Sorry," said Sam, "but at least I've worked out how to finish the levitation spell.

"I think that that's enough spells for today," said Mandy.

"I don't," replied Sam, "I can see that magic is going to be so much fun!"

"I can't wait until school starts again," said James.

"School? What about going into weight lifting?" cried Sam. "You lift the weights, I levitate them – we'll be famous."

"What about football or basketball?" said James.

"Brilliant!" they both cried, giving each other high fives.

"It's all a game to you two isn't it?" said Mandy. "Don't you think that you could do anything good with this magic?"

"Like what?" asked Sam.

"How about lifting fallen trees from off cars, clearing rock falls in mines, putting out fires."

"Putting out fires?" asked Sam, puzzled.

"You could lift up a load of water and drop it onto the fire," said Mandy wearily. "Honestly you shouldn't be doing magic if you're going to be that stupid."

"Watch who you're calling stupid – I could turn you into a toad."

"Or change you from a toad into a human," smirked James.

"Oh shut up James," said Mandy.

"Or what will you do?" asked James.

"James, *shut up*!"

Mandy picked up the cushion and threw it at James. James ducked and the cushion flew towards a picture hanging from the far wall. Sam meanwhile, had been trying the spell for levitation again. She had just finished saying 'avatar' as Mandy threw the cushion. Sam hurriedly pointed her finger at the cushion which stopped in mid air. She willed the cushion closer before rapidly moving her hand to point at James. The cushion hit James, knocking him out of the way. Sam then swung her arm round to point at Mandy, whilst at the same time saying: 'djenimi'. The cushion, suddenly out of Sam's control, flew through the air and struck Mandy in the face.

"Stop arguing you two," said Sam placidly.

"Sam, if you ever do that again I shall personally . . . do something truly hideous to you," said James.

"Me too," agreed Mandy, "honestly Sam, is this all you are going to do with magic?"

Chapter 3

"Yeah, it's unfair using magic to do things like that," said James.

"Okay, calm down," Sam said, "I was only mucking around."

"Well don't," replied Mandy.

Same spent the day reading some of the spell book, but also watching television with her brother and sister. Come night time she was tired after the events of the day. Also, although she couldn't explain why, she felt as if practising magic had made her even more tired. Nevertheless, that didn't stop her waking in the early hours of the morning.

At first, Sam just lay there and wondered to herself what had awoken her. A noise perhaps? Suddenly there was a hoarse cough from somewhere to her left, near to the window. Sam held her breath.

Suddenly, the voice which had coughed spoke:

"I can see that you are awake Samantha," it said in a reedy voice, "I have quite good night vision you know."

"Who are you?" asked Sam, trying to keep the shaking from her voice.

"I have come to visit you Samantha," replied the voice, "regarding a meeting of all the supernatural entities in England."

"What about it?" said Sam.

"It is being held here, in this village," answered the voice, "and now that you have started practising magic, you too have the privilege of attending."

"When is it?" asked Sam.

"Tomorrow night, at the large, old and seemingly abandoned house at the edge of the village green," replied the voice. "There will be only around a hundred attending – there are fewer supernaturals than you'd think in this country and quite a few of us are ghosts."

"Ghosts?"

"Yes, mainly the ghosts of dead mages who choose to stay on Earth," said the voice, "Like me."

The owner of the voice stepped forward, revealing a semi-transparent figure of a man, wearing what looked like a robe.

"I hope you attend Samantha," he said, "it's normally a fun occasion and a young witch like you could learn a lot."

"I'm a witch?" asked Sam.

"Certainly," replied the ghostly wizard, "with very good potential if I'm any judge."

There was a mumbling sound from the direction of Mandy's bed, as Mandy turned over. Sam held her breath for a second before relaxing again.

"Why is such an event being held here, in a small village like this?" asked Sam.

"Well," said the ghostly wizard, "a lot of great mages have come from around this area and besides, the meeting won't remain in the house."

"Where will it go to then?" Sam replied.

"Wherever our imaginations take us," said the wizard, "but the lead speaker will be performing most of the travelling spells."

"Who's the lead speaker?" asked Sam.

"A great wizard and the leader of our kind," replied the wizard, "none know his name."

"What is the meeting about?" asked Sam.

"Summaries of the past year from certain witches and wizards, the demonstrations of new spells from our research wizards and introducing new members into The Clan."

Sam thought for a few minutes and then said:

"I don't know. I am going out with my brother and sister tomorrow."

The wizard concentrated on something for a moment, before saying:

"You're going *trick-or-treating*? This meeting is far more important!"

"Did you read my mind?" asked Sam.

"No, I cannot read a wizardly mind, but I can read your sister's."

"Can I do that?"

"Of course," replied the wizard, "but it takes practice."

"How come you didn't use any words or use magic stones?"

"Magic stones, although useful for strengthening a spell, are not essential when you are advanced in the craft. Also, the words needn't be said when your mind becomes strong enough to say them mentally."

"Anyway," said Sam, "like I said, I'm not sure if I can . . ."

The wizard cut her off angrily:

"You act like you have a choice! To practise magic you have to be part of The Clan or you don't do it at all!"

"What?" asked Sam.

"The Clan lays down the laws of magic which every practitioner has to abide by, otherwise who can stop you attempting to rule the world?"

"I see," said Sam, "well I'll have to explain to my brother and sister . . ."

"They must not know!" cried the wizard.

"They already do know about my magic."

The wizard looked very annoyed.

"Very well, but they must be sworn to secrecy," replied the wizard. "This is most irregular, but we at The Clan are not in the habit of wiping people's minds."

"They can be sort of . . . assistants," suggested Sam.

"That seems fair enough – most of us have assistants to help us out with certain spells occasionally," said the wizard, "but they cannot attend the meeting."

"Okay."

"And now I must go. The meeting starts at nine o'clock promptly."

"Not midnight?"

"Why midnight?"

"Oh, no reason. By the way – what do I call you?"

"My name? My name is Cornelius Brown."

"Pleased to meet you Mr Brown."

"The pleasure," replied Cornelius, "is all mine."

He snapped his fingers and vanished, with a pop.

Sam sat there in silence for a few seconds thinking. Then, with a shrug, she turned over and went back to sleep.

Chapter 4

The next morning Sam awoke early, despite the disturbance in the night. At first, although she knew something had happened in the night, she couldn't recall what. Slowly, she remembered the meeting with the wizard – surely it had been a dream? After all, she had been thinking about magic a lot yesterday, what with discovering the spell book and trying out spells. Perhaps that had been a dream as well?

There was a groan from Mandy's bed as she awoke and sat up, rubbing her eyes.

"What a dream," she said in a sleepy voice.

She looked over at Sam and saw that she was awake.

"I dreamt that you learnt how to do magic Sam."

Mandy giggled to herself, clearly showing that she hadn't quite got a grip back on reality yet after being asleep.

"I did," replied Sam, "it wasn't a dream."

"Ha, ha," replied Mandy, yawning again.

"It's true," said Sam.

"Okay," replied Mandy, "what happened?"

"I made an illusion of a ball and I levitated a cushion," answered Sam.

"How did you . . ." Mandy began, before stopping and looking at Sam, "it really *did* happen?"

"Yes," said Sam. "But Mandy, I've got something important to tell you."

"What's that?" asked Mandy.

"Someone came into our room last night . . ."

"Who?"

"Let me finish – a ghostly wizard appeared in the room, telling me that to continue doing magic I have to be part of 'The Clan'."

"What's 'The Clan'?"

"A sort of . . . a sort of group of all the magic people in the country."

"How do you join?" asked Mandy.

"I go to their annual meeting."

"When's that and where?"

"Tonight at an old house at the edge of the green."

"Are you going?"

"There's not much choice, if I want to be a witch."

"But doesn't it sound a bit, you know, suspicious?"

"A bit," replied Sam, "but if that's so, why didn't

the wizard do something last night?"

"That's true," said Mandy, "but the meeting is being held in an old house."

"So?"

"Haven't you seen the horror films, where they go into the house, the door creaks open by itself and the ghost jumps out?"

"Yes, but that doesn't happen in real life though."

"I hope you're right."

"I know I'm right," said Sam, although she did have a slight feeling of foreboding. "Come on, let's have some breakfast."

In the kitchen, they were the first two to be up and about in the house. The girls made their breakfasts and then went into the lounge to watch television. An hour later James came in with his breakfast and sat down to eat it in the front of the television.

"What are we going to be doing today?" he asked.

"I want to try more of those spells," said Sam.

"Tell him about last night," said Mandy.

"What happened last night?" asked James.

Sam told him about the meeting and all the implications about being a witch.

"Are you sure you want to go?" he asked.

"Of course," Sam replied, "and as we're out trick-or-treating Mum and Dad won't even know."

"We're coming with you then," said Mandy.

"You can't – they said you couldn't."

"You can't go alone!"

"I can and I will."

"What will we do?"

"Go trick-or-treating."

"When will the meeting end?"

"I don't know – late I guess."

"What will we tell Mum and Dad?"

"I don't know – anything."

"I know what you could do . . ." said James slowly.

"What?" asked Sam and Mandy together.

"Well, you know that illusion spell that you did . . ."

"Yes?"

"You could make an illusion of yourself which would follow us around and stuff."

"Brilliant!" cried Sam.

"Hang on," said Mandy. "What if Mum and Dad speak to you?"

"I don't know – maybe I could make it talk?"

"Okay, if you get it to talk, what about touching things?"

"What do you mean?"

"Remember what happened to the ball when you touched it – it disappeared," said Mandy. "Also, what if Mum or Dad ask you to pass the salt at dinner or something, then what?"

"I don't know about not being able to pick things up," replied Sam, "But the image disappeared when *I* touched it – perhaps when other people touch it it doesn't disappear?"

"Why don't you try it?" asked James.

"Okay," said Sam, "but first, check that Mum and Dad are still in bed."

James went over to his parents bedroom and listened at the door – silence. He went back into the lounge.

"No sound at all – I think they're asleep."

"Okay, here goes," said Sam, pulling the bag of stones from her pocket. She lifted the red 'Rune' stone from the bag and proceeded to make the pentagon in the air, whilst saying:

"Addi, cysti, adonis, crytis, chi."

"Well remembered," said James, impressed.

Sam closed her eyes and imagined herself. Slowly an image appeared in front of her. It looked similar to Sam but:

"Sam, Mum and Dad are going to know that's not you," said Mandy.

"Why?" asked Sam, opening her eyes.

"It's too . . . I don't know, too perfect."

"Perfect?"

"It's probably the image of yourself that you see in your mind, with all the bad bits removed – try again."

Sam suddenly noticed the tall mirror on the wall. She walked over to it and, focusing on the reflection of herself, she tried again to project an illusion of herself. Slowly, the illusion disappeared and then reappeared. It looked just like Sam.

"There I've done it," she said, wiping the sweat from her forehead.

"It's very . . . good," said Mandy, giggling slightly.

"What's wrong with it?" Sam asked.

"Nothing, nothing," replied Mandy. "It's a perfect mirror image of you."

"So why are you laughing?"

"Can't you see? It's a *mirror image* of yourself – it's you in reverse."

"Reverse?"

"Look, you're right handed, yes?"

"Yes."

"Well it's left handed if you see what I mean."

Suddenly Sam realised what was wrong.

"I see, my mind has made the illusion of what I saw in the mirror."

Chapter 4

"By Jove, I think she's got it," said James. "Honestly you're so stupid Sam."

"Watch it or I might turn you into a toad," said Sam. "Anyway, I think I know what to do."

"What?" asked Mandy.

"Watch and learn."

Sam focused on the illusion and slowly, it melted away, before reappearing again, but this time the right way around.

"Sam, it's all very fine," said Mandy, "but the back is wrong – it doesn't look quite like you – try again."

Sam sighed and stood with her back to the mirror and looked at the rear of herself.

"I can't see the back of my head though," she said.

"Leave that to me," said Mandy, leaving the room and returning a minute later with a travel mirror. She handed it to Sam who looked at the reflected reflection of the back of her head, before turning back to the illusion, who was standing in the same place still, occasionally blinking. Sam once again imagined the image of herself until after concentrating for a few seconds, the illusion changed once more to become almost exactly like Sam.

"At last, it's right," said Mandy with relief, "but can I touch it?"

She put her hand out to touch the image, but it went straight through. Fortunately, it didn't dissolve like the ball had when Sam touched it.

"You touch it Sam," said James, after having a go himself.

Sam leant forward and touched the image of herself. The image remained the same.

"I think that I have to actually want to make it disappear," she said. "Anyway, I'm a rather attractive woman aren't I?"

"Yes, whatever," said Mandy.

"So how are you going to move it then?" asked James.

"I knew you were going to ask me that and fortunately I noticed a section in the spell book about animation," replied Sam. "It could be about one of two things – one, it is a section all about how to make a cartoon, or two, it is a section about animating objects with magic."

"I go for number one," said James.

"Well you would, wouldn't you James," replied Mandy. "Go on Sam, show us the spell then."

Samopened the spell book at the correct page and began reading the spell. After a while she said:

"There are several variations, but the one we need is the one concerning giving objects human qualities."

Chapter 4

"Can you call an illusion an object?" asked Mandy.

"It makes itself clear that you can mix spells to a certain extent so I would say yes," replied Sam.

"Carry on," said Mandy.

"The way I see it, the spell to give human qualities to objects is quite straightforward and fortunately you don't need the ingredients."

"That's a relief," said James.

"Also I can sort of copy my personality to things as well," continued Sam, "meaning that this illusion could become a sort of untouchable clone of me."

"Brilliant," said James sarcastically, "two Sams– I can't wait."

"The thought scares me as well," said Mandy. "But what the heck – go ahead Sam."

Sam pulled the blue 'Pikez' stone from the bag, replacing the Rune stone at the same time. She drew the pentagon, uttered the spell and suddenly the illusion, jerked, shook it's head and said:

"I didn't think that would work."

"Nor did I," said Sam.

"Well done, Sam," replied the clone, "I'll keep Mum and Dad off the scent and you go to that meeting tonight."

"Thanks," said Sam.

"I can't believe it," said Mandy, "That's incredible!"

"I know," said James, "I've got the feeling that this is going to be a nightmare – I mean *one* was bad enough – but*two*? Enough said!"

Suddenly they heard the sound of their parents' door opening.

"Quick – get rid of your clone," hissed Mandy.

"You're not going to get rid of me just yet," said the Sam clone, "I'm staying for a bit longer."

"Well hide then," said James.

The clone hopped behind the sofa, just before Dad entered. Sam had fortunately stuffed the book and the bag of stones deep into her dressing gown pockets.

"Morning," said Dad, "anyone want a nice cup of tea?"

"Yes please Dad," said Sam.

"And me," said James.

"I don't want any, thanks," said Mandy.

As Dad went into the kitchen, the clone came out from behind the sofa.

"Don't I get any?" she asked.

"No," said James, "You're an illusion."

"Not any more, I think, I exist."

"That's true," said Sam, "No-one's getting rid of me."

"But she's not really real," said Mandy.

"She is now," replied Sam, "although a different name wouldn't go amiss."

"How about Sam Mark Two," suggested James

"How about my middle name, Katherine?" said the clone.

"Okay then, you're Kate."

"Do you want me to make an illusion of a cup of tea for you Kate," said Sam.

"Okay," said Kate, "thanks."

"This is so weird," said Mandy.

"I know," replied James.

"Well how do you think it is for me?" asked Sam and Kate together.

"I can see your point," said James.

"Couldn't you make me look a little different after today?" asked Kate.

"After today you're going," said James.

"No way," said Kate.

"*You* tell her Sam," said Mandy, "she's going after today."

"Me?" asked Sam, "I'm keeping her."

"Yeah, and after we perfect this old magic business perhaps you could make me a bit more solid," said Kate.

"Definitely," said Sam.

"I can't believe this," said Mandy, "she can't stay."

"I can and I will," said Kate.

"Fine, okay, if you insist," said Mandy, "How about you James?"

"We can't stop them so what choice do we have."

"Where will she stay though?" asked Mandy.

"Anywhere," replied Kate.

"Anywhere?"

"Yeah, in a match box, a shoe box, in a drawer."

"If you're happy with that then fine," said Mandy.

"Look," said Sam walking through the door, "You three get acquainted , I need the toilet.'

Only thirty seconds after Sam had gone out of the room, Dad came in, carrying two hot cups of tea.

"Here you go," he said, handing a cup to James, "and here's yours Sam."

Dad held the cup out to Kate. Kate went to take the cup before remembering that she couldn't.

"I've, er, just got to go to the toilet," she said, quickly exiting the room, "Just leave it on the table."

Dad put the cup on the table, before walking out again and returning to his room, calling out:

"Be quick Sam, I need to get washed."

Chapter 4

"Okay Dad," called out Sam and Kate together.

"How did you do that?" asked Dad, stopping in the doorway.

There was silence as Sam and Kate both waited for the other to answer.

"Sam?"

Sam came out of the bathroom and saw Kate hiding around the corner. Sam put her finger to her lips and said:

"What Dad?"

"Oh, nothing," replied Dad, "You just sounded like two people, that's all."

"What do you mean?" asked Sam innocently.

"It sounded as though . . ." began Dad, before thinking better of it and saying, "It doesn't matter."

"Okay, whatever," said Sam, going into the lounge, followed shortly by Kate.

"That was too close," said Mandy.

"Dead right," agreed Sam, "we can't let anything like that happen again – we've got to be careful."

She turned to Kate.

"When Mum or Dad call 'Sam', don't answer, Kate."

"Okay, okay," replied Kate, "I'm sorry, force of habit – I keep forgetting that I'm now called Kate."

"That's alright – anyway, about tonight – what shall we do?"

"We've got a plan haven't we?" said Mandy. "Kate pretends to be you and you go off to your stupid meeting."

"Yes," said Sam, ignoring the 'stupid', "but remember what you said earlier on, about touching things?"

"Yeah, but what can we do?"

"Perhaps Kate can levitate stuff really close to her hands so it looks like she's touching things."

"Kate can't touch the stones though, how can she do the spell?" asked James.

"By doing the spell without the stones."

"But you need the stones to do the spell," said Mandy.

"Says who?" asked Sam.

"The book."

"The book doesn't actually," replied Sam, "It just emphasises their dangers. I think that the stones are there merely to add strength to the words."

"The wizard told you that didn't he?"

"He might have . . ."

"What else did he say?"

"He said that to do it you have to be advanced in the craft and you can also mentally say the words when you're good enough."

Chapter 4

"Hopeless!" said Mandy.

"Why?"

"You've only been doing magic for a day – that's hardly advanced."

"I reckon I could get Kate to do it by tonight, if we practise," replied Sam, "after all, the wizard did say that I had potential."

"Potential yes, not years of experience."

"Well I think that I can do it."

"If you say so . . ."

"I say so – and being a witch, my words have power – if I say I can, I will."

"Okay then, you'd better start now."

"Okay, Kate, let's go."

Chapter 5

And so Sam and Kate began practising the levitation magic. They decided to do it in the privacy of Sam and Mandy's room, as they didn't want their parents to suddenly walk in and find two Sams, one of them practising levitation, with a magic stone or otherwise.

First of all, they practised lifting things without the magic 'Pikez' stone. Although it was a strain mentally, both Kate and Sam were lifting items with less and less conscious effort, until they felt ready to progress onto performing the spell without uttering the words.

"Okay then Kate," said Sam, "try the spell without saying the words."

"Alright Sam," replied Kate, before closing her eyes, concentrating and saying the spell to herself in her head. She opened her eyes, focused upon the compact disc case laying upon Sam's bed and pointed her finger at it. Nothing happened.

"Djenimi," she said, ending the spell just in case it was still active.

"Try again Kate."

"Okay."

Again Kate said the words in her head, 'Chelon, levita, greyshun, avatar' and again, nothing happened. The compact disc case remained on the bed in exactly the same place.

"Hopeless," sighed Kate.

"We have to keep trying Kate," said Sam, "Let me try."

Sam tried in the same manner as Kate – after all, she was the same person – and nothing happened.

After an hour's worth of failed attempts, they were no closer to lifting the cassette case without saying the words. In fact, they found the effort of trying to lift the cassette case physically exhausting.

"I need some food," said Sam, "I'm completely drained."

"Me too," said Kate, "what have we got to eat?"

"Well Kate, as you're me, you will know that I don't know what there is to eat and also, you can't eat anyway."

"What shall I do to get back some energy?"

"I could try making the illusion of food," suggested Sam.

"Would that actually work though?"

"I made that tea didn't I?"

"Yes but I don't know if that actually nourished me or anything."

"What do you mean?"

"I just drank the illusion of the flavour of a cup of tea."

"How did you know that and I didn't?" asked Sam.

"Because I drank the tea."

"Okay," said Sam, not wishing to pursue the matter any further, "but perhaps I can strengthen the spell somehow, re-say it or something."

"Possibly," replied Kate, "But also you may strengthen the spell with the illusion of food, if I eat it with the right frame of mind – or perhaps you could give me the illusion of nutrition with the food."

"Whatever you need to give you energy, I'll have to have some food first," said Sam, "or else I'll collapse with exhaustion."

At that moment, James came in.

"Hi, we're having lunch now Sam, are you coming?"

"How did you know who was who?" asked Sam.

"Because . . ." began James, "I don't know, you looked more real I guess."

"More real?"

"Yeah," replied James, before suddenly realising what was wrong with Kate and saying, "It's because Kate is slightly see-through."

"My word, yes," said Sam in alarm, "you weren't like that earlier."

"I think all that magic I've been doing has exhausted me in a different way to you Sam," said Kate, "In fact, I think it's wearing your spell down."

"Look, I think I can manage another spell," said Sam, "but only with a magic stone."

She pulled the Rune stone from the bag and prepared herself for the spell, as Kate grew clearer and clearer. Already her hands were almost nonexistent.

"Addi, cysti, adonis, crytis, chi," said Sam, drawing the pentagon in the air with the stone. She focused upon the rapidly diminishing body of Kate and willed it to become solid looking..

"Quick Sam!" cried Kate, "I can feel my-self… go-inggggg…"

By now Kate could barely be seen at all, and Sam, sweat glistening on her forehead, concentrated on making her clone non-transparent once more. Suddenly Kate stopped disappearing and slowly she returned to normal again.

"Phew, I though I was a goner there," said Kate, "thanks Sam."

"You would have done the same."

"I know – I'm you."

"Y'know," began Sam, "I think the magic stones are there so that you use their energy instead of you using your own energy."

"Deep," said James sarcastically, "very deep and interesting, but it's lunch Sam."

Reluctantly, Sam left the room, leaving Kate to carry on practising the levitation spell now that she had her energy back.

After the much needed lunch, Sam went back into her bedroom, to find Kate still trying to attempt the spell mentally.

"No luck?" asked Sam.

"No," replied Kate, "It's hopeless, it really is."

"It's a shame that, because we're going to be in trouble if you're expected to pick anything up."

"I know."

Just then, James and Mandy came in.

"Got it to work yet?" Mandy asked. "I've been dying to know all through lunch."

"We can do it without the stone but we can't do

the spell without saying it."

"I told you," said Mandy.

"That's not helpful, Mandy."

"Okay, but I know what you can do so you don't need to keep doing the spell in your head."

"Kate can't keep saying the words every time she is expected to pick something up," said Sam, "even if she whispers it, Mum and Dad are bound to notice."

"Did I say keep on doing the spell?" asked Mandy.

"Well, what else is there to do then?"

"Don't keep on the doing the spell."

"Eh?"

"Say the spell before you go this evening and don't say the spell-finishing word, gemini or whatever it is, each time you want to put something down."

"That could work you know," said Sam.

"I see what you mean," said Kate.

"One problem though," said Sam.

"What?" asked Mandy.

"How do you let someone else move the object after you've levitated it?"

"Easy – have the spell already said, then just end it when Mum or Dad want the item – they won't notice one word," said Mandy. "When they've gone

Chapter 5

or you get a moment to yourself, you can say the words again until next time you need them."

"Brilliant idea," said Kate, "only my sister could have come up with such a stupidly brilliant plan."

"Okay, okay Kate, don't get too carried away."

"Come on, Kate let's practise now," said Sam, "Pick up the CD case like you would normally pick it up."

"Okay let's see if I can," replied Kate, "Chelon, levita, greyshun, avatar."

She leant forward and put her hands around the compact disk case so it looked like she was grasping it. She had her hand positioned so that her index finger was bent to point at the case. Kate lifted her hand, with the compact disk case apparently grasped in it. She moved her hand away and left the case suspended there in midair.

"Well done Kate," said James, "looked almost real."

"Is that sarcasm?" Kate asked.

"Who? Me?" asked James innocently. "Of course not!"

"Oh well, at least it can be done," said Sam, "I wonder if I can finish the spell for you?"

"The book says that only the person performing the spell can finish it," said Kate.

"Yes, but what if the person performing the spell is

the same as the other person finishing it?" asked Sam.

"Okay then go ahead and say it."

"Djenimi," said Sam.

The case wobbled and shook violently and the plastic began to crack and shatter into splinters which then began shaking and wobbling themselves whilst still suspended in the midair.

"You've confused it or something," cried Mandy, "Kate, say the word – quick!"

"Denimi, no djemini, sorry, djenimi!"

Suddenly the shattered case shopped shaking and dropped, whilst splinters of case flew in every direction. Fortunately, everyone apart from Kate had dived behind Sam's bed, avoiding the plastic shrapnel. Kate was unaffected, as the plastic sailed straight through her.

"Well I know now not to do that again," said Sam, "it's lucky that we didn't do that accidentally earlier today."

"I wonder why the spell went like that," said Kate, "Mandy said we confused it – perhaps because the sound of your voice is the same as mine, the spell responds to it, but I am actually channelling the magic."

"Anyway, let's hope that doesn't happen again," said Sam. "Perhaps later I could change your voice or something . . ."

"Possibly, although I do like my voice," said Kate. "It won't feel the same hearing a different sound of voice."

"Also, maybe you may want me to change your looks . . ." suggested Sam, "after all, they are very similar to mine and it is weird talking to yourself."

"No way," replied Kate, "I couldn't stand looking like someone else."

"Suit yourself," replied Sam, "Anyway, better carry on practising picking things up."

The rest of the afternoon was spent practising the spell to make it look as though she were holding items, until Kate had perfected it down to a fine art. Their parents had gone out for a walk around the village, so disturbances didn't attract attention.

By seven o'clock, Mum and Dad were back and dinner was ready. After dinner, Sam, Mandy, James and Kate were getting ready to go out trick-or-treating. The plan was that the four would go trick-or-treating for about an hour, whilst making their way to the village green and the house where the meeting was to be held. When Sam had gone, the plan was for Kate, Mandy and James to continue trick-or-treating and then to go home, where Kate would pretend to be Sam. If all went to plan, Sam would sneak in later through the window.

Sam, Mandy and James left via the front door whilst Kate left unseen through the wall of Sam and Mandy's bedroom. Sam, Mandy and James met Kate down the road and the four set off. Sam and Kate, now fully capable of levitation, were planning a few good tricks they could play, such as levitating wigs off of people's heads and levitating garden gnomes onto rooftops.

The three began trick-or-treating at ten past eight. As they scurried from door to door, they could see others also out trick-or-treating. As their bags filled, the time grew closer and closer to nine o'clock, until at five minutes to nine, they stood outside the house, which appeared to be deserted. The windows were dark and seemed to absorb the light from the street lamps instead of reflecting it. Mandy, James and Kate watched Sam as she walked up the long and overgrown path to the looming front door.

"Are you sure this is the house?" whispered Mandy to Kate.

"Yes, it's the only one which fits the description," replied Kate.

The three waiting at the gate watched as Sam went to pull back the doorknocker, but the door opened, seemingly by itself. They watched Sam enter before the door shut behind her, again seemingly by itself.

"Well that's it then," said James. "Nothing we can do now."

"Let's wait here a while before going," said Mandy.

"Okay," agreed Kate.

The three hung around by the gate for five minutes, but nothing happened.

"I say we go now," said Kate, "I can't see anything happening now."

"Okay," replied Mandy, reluctantly, "let's carry on trick-or-treating."

The three set off to trick-or-treat again, but they only did so halfheartedly, feeling that they were missing the real excitement.

"Sam's so lucky, being the magical one," said James, "I wish I could do it."

"It is a brilliant gift to have," agreed Kate, "but don't get too upset over it – Sam has to go to the meetings and things."

"Well I think I would as well," said James, "if I had the chance of doing magic."

"What's it like doing magic Kate?" asked Mandy.

"Brilliant, absolutely fantastic," replied Kate, "but I would prefer to be able to touch things still."

"What do you mean still?" asked Mandy, "You've never been able to touch."

"I am still Sam, remember, I do have the same memories up until the point that she made me. In a way, it feels as though I suddenly broke away from Sam and I suddenly became a separate person."

"How can you bear it?" asked Mandy.

"It's not too bad, I can still touch illusions and things, and one day I'll make myself solid."

"Come on," said James, "here's another house to go to."

And so the three continued trick-or-treating, until they finally got home at a little past ten o'clock.

Chapter 6

Sam heard the door close behind her. There was silence, save for the creaking of the timber in the house. All around Sam was pitch black and what light came in through the windows barely illuminated anything. Behind her, Sam began to be aware of a presence and the regular sound of deep breathing. Suddenly, a hand rested upon her shoulder. Sam yelped and spun around, before jumping back. She bumped into another figure, who tried to grab her. Sam leapt forward again, into the waiting arms of the first figure. All around her was the sound of unseen figures clambering around the large hallway chaotically. There was the sound of many voices shouting and crying out before Sam heard someone shout:

"For crying out loud, someone make some light!"

Shortly, a dull glow illuminated the hallway, into which were crowded around one hundred people, many dressed in robes. As soon as the light appeared, everybody calmed down a little. The person who had lain a hand upon her shoulder had been the wizard from the previous night, Cornelius Brown.

"Ah, young Samantha," he beamed, "creating quite a stir I see."

"Sorry about that," replied Sam, "I'm afraid that I got a bit freaked out at the spookiness of this place – why are we all waiting in the dark?"

"We await the leader of The Clan, who will unlock the doors to enter the five-sided room."

"Why can't you magic the doors open?" asked Sam.

Cornelius looked shocked.

"Because of tradition, young sorceress," he said, "and also because they are protected by the strongest and most impenetrable spells known to all magic users."

"Someone had better get rid of the light," said a person, "you know he likes us to wait in darkness."

"Good grief, yes" said the wizard who had performed the light spell. He waved his right hand and the light faded, leaving the room completely dark again.

The room waited in silence before suddenly, a great, echoing voice boomed to the assembled group:

"Welcome once again, to the one thousand five hundredth annual meeting of The Clan. As most of you are aware, I, the Leader of The Clan, shall be summarising Clan achievements over the past year, as well as presenting the forthcoming year's agenda. Also, we shall be once again taking the tour through the five magical dimensions and introducing new members to The Clan. Please make your way into the five-sided room and take a seat."

The hundred or so various magical people began filing into the dimly candlelit five-sided room, which had an old wooden table with five sides that ran parallel to the walls. The table wasn't solid all the way across, but rather it formed the outline of a pentagon and Sam was beginning to wonder whether the number five was at all significant to these people. She followed Cornelius Brown to his seat. Cornelius motioned for Sam to sit next to him and Sam did so. The table was laid out for a magnificent feast and silverware was in great abundance. In the space inside the five sides of the table was another table, also with five sides, on which there was food of every type. Sam wondered how such a large and strangely-shaped room could exist in a house which, although large, didn't look big enough to accommodate it. She nudged Cornelius, forgetting that he was a ghost. Nevertheless, Sam felt her elbow touch the ghostly mage, who looked around at her.

"Do you want something Samantha?" he asked.

"Yes," replied Sam, "I don't understand how such a big room fits in this house – it's twice as big as the ground floor looks from outside, and the ceiling is nearly as high as the house itself."

"Ah," replied Cornelius, "what you are witnessing is Heindelburg's dimensional manipulation at work."

"Magic?" asked Sam.

"Of course," said the wizard.

"I can't believe I didn't think of that," said Sam, "after all, this is a magical meeting."

She sat in her soft and comfortable chair, looking around the room at all of the members of The Clan. They ranged from ghosts to live people but all had magical ability in common. She wondered who was going to serve the food which was sitting upon the centre table still.

Suddenly, from a different door to that by which the members of The Clan had entered, came a tall figure dressed in black, with a white mask concealing its face. It took it's position at the top point of the pentagonal table and announced in the same booming voice as Sam had heard in the hallway:

"Dinner will be served shortly. Enjoy your meal,

members of The Clan, before we commence upon the first item in this evening's schedule, which is the outlining of the year's achievements, with various contributions from other members, followed by the forthcoming year's events. Second on the agenda is the welcoming of new members, followed by travelling to the five magical dimensions, where we shall once again remind ourselves of the true spirit of magic. Once again, enjoy your sumptuous meal."

From the food table, the huge dishes and serving plates suddenly lifted themselves into the air, divided into five groups consisting of the same selections of food in each, and floated towards the points of the main table, moving from diner to diner in a clockwise direction. As they stopped at each diner, the diner would heap different food from the selection onto their plate and, when finished, the dishes and plates would move on. Some diners even spooned the food onto their plates using magic. Before the selection for their length of table reached them, Cornelius Brown whispered to Sam :

"By the way, before you even think of spooning your food onto your plate using magic, remember that it's looked down upon to actually utter the words – the only people who actually do so are experienced enough to levitate without saying the spell."

"Thanks for telling me," said Sam .

As the procession approached Sam , first Cornelius filled his plate, using magic. Then it was Sam 's turn. She filled her plate, although she had only had dinner hours before, and begun tucking in.

At half past ten, the Leader announced the end of the meal. He clicked his fingers and the magnificent feast disappeared, leaving the polished wood of the table bare, save for the candles running along it. The central table had also cleared, and above this there suddenly appeared a dull white globe which began to form a moving image.

"In this past year playback," began the Leader, "you can see that Mr Jackson Jones finally rid himself of the creature that was inhabiting his cellar using his own spell, the Jackson Jones Cellular Disrupter. Unfortunately, he had to use Goldstein's Instant Cleanup spell straight afterwards, as he hadn't quite got the fine tuning of his spell correct."

Around the room there were polite laughs, and Sam felt she was being left out of some big joke.

"Seriously though, Jackson deserves congratulations for inventing this particular spell – I'm sure you've all had a persistent monster of some kind or another living in your house and I'm sure you're all aware of the problem of these monsters becoming increasingly resistant to current offensive spells, so a new form of monster control is welcome. Once we get the Jackson Jones Cellular Disrupter tested and finely tuned, we will update your spell books."

Sam listened as the Leader carried on talking about breakthrough spells and the past year's achievements. The Leader the went on to talk about the coming year's agenda and certain targets they had to reach. As the Leader spoke, the globe updated itself to show images of what he was saying.

"Over the past few centuries, new members have become less frequent, so when a new member does join, it is a cause for celebration. May I welcome Samantha into The Clan."

The existing members clapped politely as Sam was suddenly illuminated in a circle of light, as though there was a spotlight shining upon her.

"I'm sure you will go on to become a valuable member of The Clan, Samantha," said the Leader, before saying: "And Samantha is already showing a lot of promise, so keep your eyes on her!"

The light winked off and the Leader continued:

"Now that you've met Samantha, now is the time to visit the five magical dimensions again."

The Leader clicked his fingers and suddenly the

scene vanished, but instead of appearing upon some strange new world, Sam remained in the same room, but without the rest of The Clan there. The table was gone, replaced by a heavy iron cage which completely surrounded Sam , above as well as below. The Leader stood where he had been before and Cornelius remained too, standing outside of the cage in which Sam stood.

"Looks like the young witch fell for our little trap," cackled the Leader, "she fell for our little trap more easily than I thought."

"Well done master," said Cornelius, "with her power we shall be able to do as we please once more."

"The spell book trap was extremely cunning," said the Leader in a voice no longer booming. "We didn't even need to resort to other means to capture our little prize."

"What's going on?" demanded Sam.

"You are our prisoner," said the Leader, "we shall use your magical gift for our own means."

"But I thought that you had enough magic?" said Sam.

"Yes, but your power is stronger as you are younger, but unfortunately for you, you don't know how to channel it – we do, which is what we have been doing all along," replied the Leader.

Chapter 6

"Now we have you in our power we can do anything with it," said Cornelius, "and you are powerless to stop us."

"I particularly like the fact that you didn't try the spells with ingredients," said the Leader. "They would have worked nonetheless – you don't need things like ingredients to make a spell work, only knowledge."

"Then why include the spells at all?" demanded Sam.

"To make you feel bad about yourself afterwards, knowing that you had all that power at your disposal and you didn't use it," laughed the leader evilly.

"So if you aren't the leader of The Clan," said Sam, "who are you?"

"Ah, but I am the Leader of The Clan, but The Clan isn't the nice group you met," replied the Leader, "no, The Clan is a group of vicious and malicious witches who long ago wiped out all of you good witches."

"Why don't you rule the world then?" asked Sam.

"Because our power is weak compared to what it once was and by the time all of the good witches and wizards were defeated we didn't have enough power left to take over the world," said the Leader. "We decided to lie low until another powerful novice came along whom we could manipulate. We waited centuries to find another person who had the potential to become not only a witch or a wizard, but a powerful one."

"Centuries?" asked Sam, "how old are you?"

"With age you come to forget such things," said the old wizard, "but rest assured I am old."

"How did you defeat the good wizards then?" asked Sam.

"We used the law against them and revealed them as witches – they were hunted and killed for money by witch hunters who were also in our pay."

"How come you weren't hunted then?" asked Sam.

"Because the good wizards and witches never abused magic and did good with it – we on the other hand achieved positions of power and were safe."

"So what are you going to do to me now?" asked Sam.

"I am going to leave you in the darkest and dankest dungeon I can find, where I will channel your power until it fades. Then I will kill you, very slowly and very painfully."

"And don't even think about escape," barked Cornelius, "you are in a magically protected cage – you can't escape it."

Chapter 6

"And now I shall take you to my dungeon," cackled the Leader. He snapped his fingers, but instead of the cage suddenly being magicked to a dungeon, shadows around the room suddenly became animated, as shadow creatures, laughing and cackling evilly, oozed towards the cage. They were slightly human in shape, but were completely black and looked two dimensional. The only colour on them was their fiery red eyes, glowing malevolently like burnt embers. As they lifted the cage, still laughing and cackling evilly, the Leader cried out:

"At last! Our centuries of waiting are over! We can now for the first time unleash our power upon the world and *no-one* can stop us – *no-one*! Samantha the novice witch – behold my Clan of shadow wizards, drinking in your power, with you unable to harness it to even a *small* extent!"

"You won't do it you know!" shouted Sam, "you'll never take over the world if I can help it!"

"Ah, but you can't, so I will take over the world and everybody in it – you shall all be my slaves!" cried the wizard. "And when I control the people, I shall hand pick my apprentice wizards until nothing can stop us!"

"And what'll happen to me when you have all this power?" asked Sam, "apart from me dying a painful death in years to come when my power fades."

"You shall continue furnishing me with power so I don't get overrun by young wizards eager to overthrow me with their power," replied the Leader. "Also, you will be my exhibit of what will happen to any who disobey."

Sam was taken through the doorway, out into the hallway, carried in her cage by the shadow people. She was carried over to another doorway which led down to what Sam assumed was a cellar. She then remembered the Leader's mention of a dank and dark dungeon, and groaned. She couldn't see any way of escaping as she stood in the cage as it was carried down some wet stone steps into a pitch-black room. The cage seemed to be carried along corridors which were invisible to Sam for what seemed a long time, meaning that she was indeed in a proper dungeon and not some dank cellar. She assumed that the dungeon spread beneath a lot of the village by the distance the cage seemed to be going. Suddenly she came to a halt, and Sam was dumped unceremoniously onto the floor, and the cackling shadow people moved off, their laughter echoing eerily down the corridors. Sam was alone and by herself in the dark. She began trying to work out an escape plan, but

Chapter 6

couldn't see how she could get through the thick and magically protected bars of the cage.

Chapter 7

After only a few minutes, the dark seemed to be closing in upon Sam and she began to imagine things in the darkness outside of the cage – unspeakable horrors which lurked there, waiting any minute to pounce. Finally Sam could bear it no more.

"Addi, cysti, adonis, crytis, chi," she cried, saying the illusion spell. She concentrated until there was suddenly a soft, glowing ball of light which appeared above the cage and illuminated the surrounding dungeon with a cold white light. Sam looked around her and shuddered. The walls were covered in thick, green slime, which oozed down to the floor and accumulated in thick puddles. Rats the size of terriers scuttled over the floor, which was covered with the skeletons of dead rats and mice, as well as slime. In the distance, down one of the many corridors, Sam could make out another cage, containing a human skeleton slumped inside, with its hands still gripping the bars, as if it still hoped to escape its prison. Sam wished that she hadn't created the light, but she didn't want to turn it off now, knowing that her imagination would play tricks on her, telling her that there were noises outside the cage that weren't really there.

She had to think of a plan fast, she decided, or else spend eternity here, going insane through loneliness and terror.

The hours rolled slowly past until suddenly, Sam thought of something stupidly simple and she couldn't believe she hadn't thought of it earlier. She could create another clone of herself, or use Kate by projecting Kate's image in front of her and moving Kate from wherever she was now to here.

Sam closed her eyes and concentrated for a few seconds, manipulating the spell which had created Kate that was still active even after so many hours. Suddenly there was a brief scream in the sound of Sam 's voice. Sam opened his eyes.

"Shh!" she said.

"Where am I?" cried Kate, "and what are you doing in that cage Sam?"

"I'll be brief," said Sam, "But basically The Clan was all a sham – the meeting was an illusion and, halfway through, it disappeared, I was in this magic-proof cage and the real Clan showed up, consisting of giggling nasties made, apparently, of shadows. The Leader wants me for my magical power – it seems that he is losing his as he gets older."

"Wow!" said Kate, "you were really duped Sam."

"As were you," replied Sam.

"So how come I'm here?"

"I brought you here – I rather hoped that you might bring the spell book."

"Sorry, you should have asked," said Kate half-jokingly, "So what do you want me to do?"

"I'll send you back home for fifteen minutes, you find a spell which is appropriate and I'll levitate you back here again."

"Okay," replied Kate, "I'll find something for you."

Sam closed her eyes and concentrated on putting Kate back at the cottage in her bedroom until when she opened her eyes again, Kate had gone.

The next fifteen minutes seemed to be the slowest ever fifteen minutes Sam had ever experienced. The skeleton in the cage was really beginning to bother her and when she turned his back to it, she could feel it watching her. It was just her imagination, she told herself as she looked at her watch again. She turned around to take another look at the skeleton, but to her surprise and mounting horror, it was gone – the cage was empty. There was still five minutes left until Kate returned, and Sam found herself wanting to bring her back now. She decided to do it, in the hope that Kate had found the right spell. She tried to concentrate with her eyes wide open to bring Kate back, but couldn't do it – she was too tense and nervous to concentrate. Hearing an echoing clicking sound, similar to how Sam imagined that a walking skeleton would sound, should it be walking through a dungeon, Sam decided to utter the words to the levitation spell, just in case something should turn up. The clicking began to get louder and louder, and Sam didn't know where it was coming from. She spun round and round, looking for the approaching skeleton, but couldn't see it. She stopped turning and regained her balance as the clicking stopped and a voice by his right ear said:

"Are you looking for me?"

Sam spun around to see that the skeleton from the cage in the distance was standing behind her, in the very same cage.

"Argh!" she cried, pointing her finger at the skeleton, and lifting it to the top of the cage using the spell she had fortunately prepared.

"How did you do that!" Sam demanded.

The skeleton, although incapable of making facial expressions, looked shocked.

"Put me down! Put me down!" it cried, "You're crazy – put me down!"

"Not until you explain who you are, why you're in my cage and how you got in!"

"I'm a prisoner here – like you!" it replied frantically, "I was left here to die as I was the last good wizard alive – I used some of my magic to keep me alive, but it couldn't stop my body form rotting away, leaving my skeleton."

"Go on," said Sam, "why are you in my cage?"

"You are the first person I've seen in centuries who isn't a shadow being, I didn't mean to sneak up on you,"

"And how did you get in?" asked Sam.

"Over the centuries I managed to work out how to escape the cage by defeating its protective spells," replied the skeleton. "But, until today, I haven't been able to defeat them as I had no magic left."

"So you tapped into mine," said Sam, "why is it that every accomplished wizard I meet wants a bit of my magic?"

"If you really want an answer to that, then it's because you are one of the last young witches left, from what I have been able to sense over the years from the outside world." replied the skeletal wizard. "Also you make it rather easy for other wizards to use your power as you don't control it properly and it radiates from you, turning you into a sort magical beacon."

"How do I control the power then?" asked Sam.

"You need tutoring," replied the wizard, "I can help you, once I have a new body."

"How do you do that?" asked Sam.

"My word, you are new to it aren't you," muttered the wizard, "I shall have to teach you."

"I've only been doing magic for a couple of days," said Sam.

"A couple of days?" asked the wizard in surprise, "then you really are powerful – you shouldn't have mastered levitation, even under tuition, until at least several months of practise."

"How long will you take to create a new body then?" asked Sam, with a touch of pride in her voice.

"How long will it take you to put me down again?" asked the skeleton.

"Oh, I see, right," said Sam, "Djenimi!"

The wizard dropped to the ground with a horrible clicking, rattling noise of bone against metal.

Chapter 7

"Perhaps I should have lowered you first," said Sam.

"Yes," replied the wizard. As the wizard stood up, Sam could already see the flesh growing back and body organs growing inside the wizard's ribcage. A network of veins and arteries sprung up, joining to the now pumping heart. Sam turned away in disgust – this was perhaps the most revolting thing she had ever seen in her life.

"You can turn back now," said the wizard.

Sam turned, dreading what she might see. The wizard looked to be in his sixties, with grey hair and a long, flowing grey beard. Fortunately he had created a robe as well to cover up his newly regrown body.

"I used to lead the good wizards and witches you know," said the wizard. "Until the witch-hunting started and the good magic users perished at the hands of the witch hunters, who were in the pay of the evil wizards, ironically."

"What's your name?" asked Sam .

"Henry," replied the wizard, "Henry Balcombe."

"Well then Henry, would you mind getting me out of this cage."

"I've broken the spells on it, now do whatever you want to get out."

"How did you get in?"

"I teleported."

"Teleported?"

"Yes, transported myself into the cage."

"I think I will just bend the bars," said Sam.

"Go ahead then, but be quick."

Sam said the words of the levitation spell, thinking to herself how useful it had become, and pointed to the bars of the cage. She moved her arm right and bent the bars back, then she pointed at the adjacent bar and moved her arm left, leaving a gap between the two bars which was large enough to squeeze through.

"Okay, what now?" asked Sam .

"We teleport up," said Henry.

"How do I teleport though?"

"By saying: telepi, juanetti, ourteri and imagining where you want to go, say like outside this wretched hou…"

The wizard suddenly disappeared mid-sentence, leaving Sam alone in the dungeon. What did she have to say? Right, she had it.

"Telepi, juanetti, outeri," she said, imagining being on the common, outside the house. As she felt the dungeon slip away from her, she heard the Leader gasp as he turned the corner of the passageway and saw Sam disappearing.

Suddenly Sam was on the common, standing

about twenty metres from the house. She saw Henry looking around for him outside the house.

"He spotted me leaving!" cried Sam, "we have to escape!"

"Where?" asked Henry, turning around.

"Anywhere!" shouted Sam .

Sam ran towards the wizard and the two of them set off.

"If we're lucky, he won't know where we went," said Sam .

"And if we're unlucky?"

"He'll teleport to where we were a moment ago."

"Let me fight him," panted the wizard.

"No, your powers are too weak as it is," said Sam , "You are using my magic when you fight him – he is using my magic too but also his own."

As they rounded a corner, they heard the Leader's screech of anger as he appeared outside the house.

"Come my demons!" he shouted, "Follow me to hunt down these wretches!"

He set off in pursuit of his escapees, with shadow people following him from out of the darkness. As Sam and Henry Balcombe ran, they felt the fingers of shadow people reaching out and trying to grab their legs.

"Teleport to my house!" screamed Sam to the wizard.

"Where is it?"

"Okay, to the high street!"

The wizard mentally said the words and disappeared, followed shortly by Sam who had to say the words to the spell physically. She appeared at the other end of the high street to the wizard, so she quickly teleported down to the wizard's end.

"What now?" gasped Henry.

"I don't know, but we've at least bought some time," said Sam .

At that moment, James, Mandy and Kate turned into the high street from a side road.

"James! Mandy! Kate!" called Sam, "What are you doing here?"

James, Mandy and Kate hurried over to Sam and Henry.

"I decided to check that everything was okay when you didn't take me back to the dungeon," explained Kate. "They insisted that they come along too."

"Who's this?" asked James.

"Another wizard," replied Sam.

"Shouldn't we be running then?" asked James.

"No, he's good," replied Sam, "did you find a spell?"

"I didn't have time to look through the whole book, but I found a fireball spell," replied Kate, "I didn't find any escaping spells, but it looks like you did okay on that account."

"A fireball spell – he will shrug that off," said Henry, "I say, are you a clone of Samantha?"

"Only the illusion of clone I'm afraid."

"Can you fight him?" Sam asked Henry.

"I'll do my best, but I am not as powerful as he."

"Couldn't I prevent him from using my power?" asked Sam .

"You can try," said Henry, "but I doubt you will be able to – you need spells of protection which I haven't time to teach you."

Suddenly, at that moment, the Leader appeared down the other end of the street, now accompanied by Cornelius.

"Mandy, James – hide," cried Sam.

Mandy and James leapt into a hedgerow, as the Leader began firing balls of fire and lightning down the street at Sam , Henry and Kate.

"I see you have company Samantha," laughed the Leader evilly, "I doubt that it'll do you good – it is only a clone of you."

"We'll see," answered Sam .

"Hold your hands out like this to deflect the fireballs Samantha," said Henry.

"Henry, it is so good to see you alive and well again," sneered the Leader, "come to die again have you?"

Henry made a complicated motion with his hands, sending a shaft of lightning at the Leader. The Leader deflected it easily and returned a green fireball, which went straight through Kate.

Kate said a word of power which sent the fireball spell she had learnt at the unsuspecting Cornelius, who ducked just in time. Cornelius cast a spell to run molten lead inside Kate's bones, not realising that Kate didn't have any bones. Henry cast a spell which made a hundred ravens appear and bear down upon the Leader with the intent to peck him to death. The Leader fired a huge ball of fire at them, cooking them alive. The leader laughed maniacally as the roasted carcasses of the birds fell to earth like rain. He then cast a spell which created another cage above Sam . The cage dropped like a portcullis and Sam leapt away just in time. It was obvious to her that the Leader meant to keep her alive.

All along the street, lights came on as people heard the noises in the street. Terrified townsfolk watched as the wizards battled. One had obviously telephoned the police, as in the distance came to sound of sirens.

A huge bubble of magic surrounded the wizards

as they battled with greater and greater spells. The air cooked and strange creatures were briefly summoned into existence by random bursts of magic.

The first police car arrived as Sam destroyed a group of shadow people trying to sneak up on them with the fireball spell which she had learnt from Kate. The driver of the car was so astonished, that he drove his police car into a lamp post, toppling it towards the bubble of magic. As the lamppost hit the bubble of magic it melted into a puddle of molten metal which then boiled and evaporated into nothing.

Further police cars arrived, many with armed police officers. One brave but stupid policeman tried to enter the bubble of magic and was instantly cooked alive and burnt into nothing, his brief yet terrible screams sending a shiver down the spines of the onlookers. This was the cue for the police to open fire upon the magic-brandishing fighters. A lot of the bullets melted as they hit the magical energy field. The rest of the bullets either turned into something else or were magically reflected back to where they had come from, wounding many of the policemen there. Policemen in charge of the assault who were ducking behind their police cars were frantically requesting assistance from the army over their radios.

Sam began to feel drained as she battled against the evil wizards. She felt as if every magic user in the vicinity was using her magic, which was true. She didn't feel as if she could supply the energy any more. She looked over at Kate, who was hurtling fireballs with wild abandon. Sam's clone began to flicker and warp until suddenly it disappeared with a pop. Sam caught the spell book, which Kate had been levitating, as it fell.

In the bushes, Mandy said to James:
"Kate's gone!"
"I know, but have you seen Sam?"
"My God, it's like she is becoming less real, but I can't explain it."
"I don't think she can take it any more, supplying the magic which they're all using."

Sam shook her head, trying to get rid of the grogginess which seemed to be overcoming her. The shadow people, who were about to make a massed assault suddenly disappeared, as Sam's magic faltered. Sam staggered back and collapsed onto the floor, unable to stand any more, leaving Henry to battle it out with the two other wizards. Sam lifted her hand shakily and pointed her finger at the

Chapter 7

Leader and said a magic word which launched a fireball from her fingertip. Sam's hand was shaking so much that her shot was wildly off target. She groaned as she saw it missing the Leader, but suddenly there was a tortured scream, as Cornelius, who hadn't expected any more spells from the fallen figure of Sam, was hit by the fireball intended for the Leader. Cornelius' screams continued, as he collapsed to the ground beating at the fire engulfing his body. They were abruptly cut off as the fire seemed to penetrate Cornelius' body, turning it into a giant, red hot, human shaped ember, which then collapsed into dust.

Sam looked over at Henry, whose flesh seemed to be peeling away from his skeleton as Sam's diminishing power failed to maintain the spell which had created Henry's new flesh. The skin was almost nonexistent and Sam could see Henry's organs, remaining in place only with the fading magic.

The spells which the two wizards still hurled at each other had become weaker and less spectacular as Sam's magic faded. The bubble of magic was less potent than it had been, but it was still powerful. The two duelling wizards seemed to be battling by reusing the magic surrounding them rather than using Sam's now low reserves of magic.

Although the magic was getting weaker, the two fighting wizards were also growing weaker, meaning that they didn't react so quickly to magical attacks and their magical defences were faltering.

The two remaining wizards – one good, one evil – battled away, standing their ground as the tarmac they stood upon bubbled and spat. The Leader aimed and fired a thin and concentrated line of white-hot fire at Henry's head. The wizard sluggishly raised his hand in defence and luckily deflected the fire away from him towards a hedge, which erupted into flame. Whilst the Leader prepared his next spell, the good wizard finished uttering the words of his spell which would burn the enemy wizard from the inside. A spectacular semi-translucent red spiral hissed towards the Leader who deflected it easily away from himself and at a police car which exploded, sending police officers flying in all directions. The Leader quickly finished a particularly nasty spell which would turn the good wizard's body inside out if it succeeded in hitting him. He raised his hand and sent the spell screaming towards Henry, who saw it coming and defended himself with his right hand, sending the spell blazing to his right and up, and unfortunately hitting a spectator of the battle high above at their bedroom window.

"Ugh!" said James, quickly looking away from the accident before being sick into a flower bed. Mandy looked to where James had looked and did the same.

Henry, after deflecting the latest attack from the Leader, sent one hundred jet-propelled, red hot, razor-sharp blades hurtling towards the Leader, who, finding a hidden burst of speed, rapidly made lightning-fast motions with his hands and reversed the spell which Henry had just sent at him. Henry was caught completely unawares as the red hot blades seared through his remaining flesh and tore it from his bones. Staggering back and managing to complete his next spell, Henry was able to raise his hands at the Leader, intending to erupt the ground beneath his enemy. At this point, Sam's magic levels suddenly dipped for a few seconds, causing the spell to end up as just a wisp of smoke from the wizard's fingers. The Leader, seeing his chance to follow up his deflection of the red-hot blades, raised his hands to hurl a basic ball of fire at the reeling form of Henry. Henry, who was remaining upright through great willpower looked up to see the fireball heading toward him. Shifting power from keeping his once-more skeletal figure upright towards defence was too much for Henry. As he lessened the magic holding his bones together, they fell apart, falling into a heap upon the road making a hollow sound as they hit each other. The fireball superheated the remains of Henry's skeleton, splintering them as it sailed past and continued along the road leaving a bubbling line of tarmac, before finally fading into nothing fifty metres away.

Over the next few minutes there was silence. The tarmac stopped bubbling and spitting as it cooled down. All of the onlookers were expecting something more and were waiting with bated breath for the Leader to do something, but the victorious wizard just stood there panting and swaying, overcome by his excessive use of magic over the past few hours. As the magical bubble became less intense and was partially reabsorbed into Sam's still body, it was clear that nothing was going to happen for a while yet. Conversations sprung up all over the street as people began frenzied discussions over what had just occurred. When they considered the bubble of magic to be weak enough as to be safe, James and Mandy hurried over to Sam, avoiding the Leader, and knelt down beside her. Sam's skin was pale and cold and James and Mandy feared the worse.

"The strain must have been too much for her,"

said James in a quiet voice, "they must have sucked the life out of her."

"Are you sure . . .?" asked Mandy.

"I think so," sighed James sadly.

Suddenly, Sam's eyes opened a little. She blinked once or twice and opened her eyes fully. James smiled thankfully and then gasped, as he saw that his sister's eyes, normally dark brown, had turned a pale shade of grey.

"How do you feel Sam?" asked James.

"F-feel w-weak," panted Sam, "d-did we win?"

Sam read the look on James' face and sighed.

"How c-come you two are still here," asked Sam.

"The Leader guy is just standing there – no-one is going near him," said James. "He finished your friend off in the end."

"His power is w-weak," said Sam, "kill him now while y-you still can."

"We can't," said Mandy, "he still has the power to hurl fireballs and he will use them against us."

"You've got to, it's our only hope," croaked Sam.

Suddenly, there was the sound of laughter as the Leader recovered himself.

"I have won!" he cried, "none shall stop me!"

"Kill… him," said Sam, before she blacked out once more.

James and Mandy looked up in terror as the

Leader strode over to them. They stood up and ran, knowing that the Leader wouldn't hurt Sam if he could help it, knowing that Sam still had magic which could be used.

"Her life-force is low but she will recover," said the Leader, "but I think that you two don't have anything that I require – you'll probably try to save your sister so I think that I should kill you right now."

"Hang on!" cried James, jumping out of the way of a fireball, "Life-force?"

"Yes, that's what keeps her alive."

"But surely it is her magic that is low," said James, jumping out of the way of another fireball.

"Don't you realise," said the Leader, "her magic is caused by more life-force being generated than her body needs – that is what magic is."

"Life-force?"

"Yes, but when a person with too much life-force gets older, he stops producing it at such a rate – normal people die when their body doesn't get enough life force."

"What about wizards?"

"They carry on living for many decades after a normal person would – even centuries," replied the Leader. "They still produce an excess for a lot of that time, but sadly not as much as great magic requires."

Chapter 7

"Is that why you have used Sam then?" asked James.

"It is common for older magical users to tap into younger wizards' supplies," said the Leader. "In the olden days when wizards were more common, the reason we had clans was so that the older and experienced wizards could use the younger and less experienced wizards' magic."

The Leader, who had stopped attacking James and Mandy started to again, saying:

"Enough, we have talked enough – prepare to die!"

"But surely you using Sam's magic will kill her when you have used up her life-force?" cried Mandy.

"That is a risk I am prepared to take," said the Leader, hurling fireballs at the two of them.

"Why choose evil though?" asked James.

"Power!" answered the Leader, "And the freedom to do what I want with magic, without having any laws to prevent me ruling the world!"

"But surely there are drawbacks?" cried Mandy, "Surely evil can't be all beneficial?"

"What are you getting at?" asked the evil wizard fearfully, "What do you know?"

James and Mandy realised that there must be a way of defeating the Leader now, after hearing how fearful he was.

"If you are worried for your sister's life-force," said the Leader, with renewed vigour, "I suggest you let me hit you!"

James and Mandy ran, as the half-mad wizard pursued them down the road.

"I am the greatest!" he cried, "None stand in my way – both of you will perish!"

At that moment, the sun came over the horizon, spreading the cold fingers of dawn over the landscape. As the weak sunlight fell upon the Leader, he screamed in agony and slowed down to a stop. As the horrified onlookers watched, the wizard's body began to go grey and stiffen.

"Arghhhh!" he screamed, "the accursed spell of the good – noooo!"

"What's happening?" asked James.

The Leader looked at him with hatred.

"The spell – if ever I am exposed to the light of day I am to be turned to stone – he . . ." the Leader pointed to the splinters of bones, "...did it, centuries ago."

The Leader's skin began hardening as the Leader's body turned to stone. He screamed once more for the last time and then was silent, his face contorted and his body rigid.

Chapter 8

The street was once again silent and the onlookers awaited the next incident. They gradually began talking among themselves again, feeling safe in the knowledge that nothing more was going to happen.

James cautiously approached the figure of the Leader. As he approached, it became clear that the Leader had indeed turned to stone and even looked a little ridiculous still wearing robes. James tried to push what was now nothing more than a statue but it wouldn't budge.

Suddenly, James remembered Sam and quickly he ran over to Sam's still body. Mandy hurriedly followed.

"Is she . . . ?" asked Mandy, unable to say the word 'dead'.

James felt Sam's neck with two fingers, looking

for a pulse. For a heart-stopping moment he couldn't find one, but then he felt it – faint, but still there.

Mandy saw the relieved look on James' face and smiled thankfully.

"Come on," she said, "let's get her back home."

"Wait a moment," said James, "what about Mum and Dad?"

"We'll just have to see if they have heard all this," said Mandy.

"I doubt that they have missed it," said James. "I think everyone in the village *and* the outskirts has heard it."

"Let's take her back anyway."

"What about a hospital?" suggested James. "Surely we should take her to one first?"

"Do you think she's in that bad a condition?" asked Mandy.

"We can't be sure she's okay – all that life-force that she has lost that the Leader spoke of – she might not even be the same person when she wakes up," said James, "*if* she wakes up."

"I don't want to think about it," said Mandy.

Suddenly, Sam coughed and opened her eyes a little. She tried to look into James' face, but couldn't focus.

"I f-feel t-t-terrible," said Sam shakily.

"Don't worry Sam," said James, "you're going to be all right."

"W-what happened?"

"Nothing, just stay there and relax."

Sam tried to sit up. She shifted her arms slightly but couldn't manage to push herself up on them.

In the background there suddenly came the faint sounds of ambulance sirens. Someone had obviously contacted the hospital. Many townspeople and police officers began helping the injured and digging people out from the wreckage caused by the magical battle. Over the circle of half-cooled tarmac which the magical bubble had melted, some police officers began treading their way cautiously, examining some of the things that the magic had conjured into existence. A few crouched down to examine the shards of bones which were all that were left of Henry. One approached James and Mandy.

"Is she okay?" asked the officer, looking down at Sam.

"She has trouble moving and has trouble remembering what just happened," said James, "I think she needs to be taken to hospital."

"Do you know her?" asked the officer.

"She's our sister," replied James.

"In that case, if you give me your name and telephone number, I will contact your parents and tell them the news."

Mandy gave him the telephone number of the cottage. The officer spoke into his radio, asking the station to ring the cottage at once to inform their parents of what had happened.

The policeman looked around and said:

"Will you two be okay here until the ambulances arrive? Only there are other people who are injured and need all the help they can get."

The policeman left, without awaiting a reply. After he had gone, Sam attempted to sit up again but couldn't. She lay back on the tarmac and said to her brother and sister:

"You've got to get me away from here before Mum and Dad arrive."

"Why?" asked Mandy.

"I have a plan," replied Sam.

"You remember everything then?" asked James.

"Yes – you have to be quick."

"What about hospital – you need to go there."

"Take me away before they get here as well," said Sam, "hurry!"

James and Mandy looked at each other.

"Shall we?" mouthed James.

"I don't know," replied Mandy silently.

"Don't talk over me!" cried Sam, "Believe me on this one!"

"Before we move you, does anywhere hurt?" asked James.

"No – why?" asked Sam.

"Because I don't want to move you if anything is broken."

"I didn't get hit at all," said Sam. "I had all my magic sucked from my body which is why I'm like this."

"That's good enough for me," said James, "grab his legs Mandy."

James took Sam's arms and the two of them hoisted her off of the ground and manhandled her around the corner into a side street and behind a hedge.

"We're alright here for now," said James.

"Hopefully everyone was too preoccupied to see us take her away."

"What now?" asked Mandy, looking down at Sam, who said:

"I need to rest – so . . . tired."

"You haven't got time!" cried James.

Sam shook her head slightly and said:

"No, you're right, let me think for a few moments."

Sam lay there for five minutes with her eyes

closed until James said:

"Don't go to sleep Sam."

"I'm not going to – I'm trying to work out a spell."

"Do you want the book?" asked James, who had picked it up from the road.

"I don't need the book," replied Sam, "I need to think."

After a further tense five minutes Sam opened her eyes and said:

"Okay, I am ready to do the spell."

"Are you up to it?" asked Mandy.

"No," grinned Sam, "but I'll do it anyway."

Sam, with her eyes once again closed, began to mouth a long stream of seemingly meaningless words. She did so for a few minutes until suddenly time seemed to stand still and then go backwards. Sam, James and Mandy were surrounded by another magical bubble, delicate looking and pinkly tinted. The world outside of the bubble was running backwards faster and faster, until hours went by in minutes.

After what seemed like an eternity, but was in fact barely a quarter of an hour, the pinkly tinted bubble vanished with a loud 'pop' and time seemed to be running normally again. The sky was black and hung with stars. Across the road a group of children dressed up as witches and ghosts passed by.

Chapter 8

James and Mandy looked down at Sam, who could barely keep her eyes open. She mouthed the words of the teleport spell, but with a slight variation which allowed herself, as well as her brother and sister to be teleported back to the cottage, and into Sam's room. The clock on the wall said eight o'clock.

"We're back to before the meeting is due to start," said James to Mandy, "Just after dinner."

"Will we meet ourselves?"

"I don't think Sam would allow that."

The two looked down at Sam when James mentioned her name. Sam had teleported herself onto her bed, but unfortunately it looked as though the last spell had been too much for her.

"I think that this time she really is . . ." began James.

He was stopped by Mandy shaking his arm. He looked down at Sam and was amazed at how well she suddenly looked.

"But just now she looked so . . ." he began. He was interrupted by Sam yawning as if she had just been asleep and was waking up. She looked lost for a moment and then grinned smugly.

"So it worked then," she said.

"What did?" asked Mandy.

"My last spell."

"The teleporting one?"

"No, the life force restoring one."

"You mean that you knew that this would happen?" asked James.

"Of course, but I didn't really have time to say anything."

"How did you restore your life force?" asked Mandy."

"By opening a sort of time hole from before I had my magic drained and sort of sucking magic from it," said Sam, "I wasn't too sure I would have the power to tell you the truth."

"How did you know how to do all of that?" said James.

"When the wizards were all tapping into my magic, I sort of managed to tap into their knowledge," replied Sam.

"Sam," said Mandy, "I've been wondering."

"What about?"

"If we're back to before the meeting, then that means that it will all happen again," said Mandy.

"Don't worry, I've seen to that," smiled Sam. She leant over to her bedside drawer and lifted out a can of coke. She opened it and raised it into the air, as if carrying out a toast.

"Happy Halloween!" she grinned, taking a swig from the can.

In a room which lies somewhere deep beneath the village, there is a statue. The statue wears robes which make it look too lifelike to be just a statue and the expression on the statue's face suggests that it is a statue of a man screaming out in fear. A long way above the room, on the surface and walking along the village high street, is a man, dressed in tattered, fire scorched and muddy robes, who shuffles along, looking for money in the gutter. The man is clearly a tramp. He can't remember his name any more, but he does know that it began with a certain letter – the letter 'C'.

We hope you enjoyed this story from the pen of Edgar J. Hyde. Here are some other titles in the Creepers series for you to collect:

Edgar Escapes!

The Ghostly Soldier

Blood On Tap

Dr Death

Soul Harvest

This series was conceived by Edgar J Hyde and much of the text was provided by his minions under slavish conditions and pain of death! Thankfully none of the minions defied their master and so we can say 'thank you' to them for toughing it out and making this series possible.

Doctor Death

Have you ever gone to the doctor with a minor illness only to find that you feel even worse? That's what happens to Josh Stevens and his friends. They turn from a bunch of healthy kids into smelly, greasy, pustulent wrecks - and coincidentally they have all just paid a visit to the charming and handsome Doctor Blair. Josh's hideous boils are jeopardising a future date with the lovely Karen but there are much more sinister "remedies" lurking in the good doctor's medicine cupboard. But how can Josh and his friends stop Doctor Death carrying out is deadly plan?

The Ghostly Soldier

Angus and Ishbel love to hear the stories about heroic Scottish warriors. They visit the site where the Battle of Culloden was fought and Angus romanticises the events, wishing that he could have been there to help fight the Redcoats. His opinion changes when an explosion in their garden unleashes the spirits of ghostly warriors from the battle. Angus is accidentally caught up in the terrifying world of the restless spirits of English and Scottish soldiers who must fight the battle again and again. The children must return the spirits to where they belong, but how?

Soul Harvest

The Grimaldis, a creepy new family who have a bad attitude and who dress entirely in black move into Billy and Alice's neighbourhood. Very soon afterwards their mum and dad and all the other neighbours start to act very strangely - as if they have suddenly become wicked. The children, and their friends Ricky and Alex, are soon the only normal ones left in a neighbourhood of thieves, bullies and thugs. The entire village, headed by the Grimaldi's is soon trying to find the four children and capture their souls to make the imminent 'harvest' complete!